The Yard

by Susan McCloskey
illustrated by Merle Nacht

HOUGHTON MIFFLIN COMPANY

BOSTON

ATLANTA   DALLAS   GENEVA, ILLINOIS   PALO ALTO   PRINCETON

Mom and Dad Carter liked to go to
yard sales. The kids did, too.
They had lots of fun finding nice things.
And they all just loved a bargain.

They got a sofa with a missing leg.
What a bargain!
"I can fix this," said Dad.
"It will look good in our living room."

But Dad never had time to fix the sofa.
So it just sat in the garage.

They got an old doll carriage.
What a bargain!
"This will be great to put plants in," said Mom.
"All it needs is a little paint."

But Mom never had time to
paint the doll carriage.
So it just sat in the garage.

They got a little swimming pool.
What a bargain!
"This will be fun for the
kids when it gets hot," said Dad.

But the little swimming pool had a
little hole in it. So it just sat in
the garage, too.

yard sale

10

They got a tall lamp.
What a bargain!
"The shade is torn," said Mom. "But I can
always patch it."

But Mom forgot to patch the shade.
So the lamp just sat in the garage with
all the other stuff.

Dad got a painting. What a bargain!
"I can give this to my friend Al for
his birthday," Dad said.
"All it needs is a new frame."

But Dad never got a new frame.
So into the garage went the painting.

They got an elephant. It was free!
"This is the biggest bargain of all," said Mom.
"We'll keep it in the garage until
I sew on a new ear."

But there was no room in the garage.

"What are we going to do with
  all this stuff?" asked Mom.
"I know what we can do," Dad said.
"We can have a yard sale!"